MOUSE'S FIRST NIGHT AT
MOONLIGHT SCHOOL

First published 2014 by Nosy Crow Ltd
The Crow's Nest, 10a Lant Street, London SE1 1QR
www.nosycrow.com

This edition published 2015 for Scottish Book Trust

ISBN 978 0 85763 595 2

Nosy Crow and associated logos are trademarks and/or registered trademarks of Nosy Crow Ltd

Text © Simon Puttock 2014
Illustrations © Ali Pye 2014

The right of Simon Puttock to be identified as the author and Ali Pye to be identified
as the illustrator of this work has been asserted.

A CIP catalogue record for this book is available from the British Library.

Printed in China

Papers used by Nosy Crow are made from wood grown in sustainable forests.

1 3 5 7 9 8 6 4 2

FOR ALL OUR SMALLER SELVES
S.P.

FOR MUM AND DAD, WITH LOVE
A.P.

MOUSE'S FIRST NIGHT AT MOONLIGHT SCHOOL

SIMON PUTTOCK
Illustrated by ALI PYE

nosy crow

This is Miss Moon's Moonlight School
for all the wee small creatures of the night.

The night bell was about to ring,

and Bat

and Cat

and Owl were all on their way.
But somebody was missing and
that somebody was . . .

...Mouse!
It was Mouse's very first night at Miss Moon's Moonlight School, and Mouse was feeling shy. So she had come in extra early and hidden behind the curtains.

"Has anyone seen our new pupil?"
asked Miss Moon.
"Has anyone seen Mouse?"
Owl put up his wing.

"Yes, Owl?"
asked Miss Moon.

"I have not seen
Mouse," said Owl.

Cat put up her paw.
"I have sadly not seen
Mouse either," she said.

"Bat," asked Miss Moon,
"have YOU seen Mouse?"

"Oh no, Miss Moon," said Bat.
"I have never seen Mouse EVER!"

"How mysterious,"
said Miss Moon.
"Mouse, dear,
are you here?"

Now, Mouse's mother had said to Mouse, "Be sure to be good," so . . .

. . . "I AM here," said Mouse
in a VERY small voice,
a voice too small to be
properly heard.

"Did somebody
say something?"
Miss Moon asked.

"I said it!" shouted Mouse.
"And I am HIDING because I am SHY."

"But WHO, and WHERE are you?"
asked Miss Moon.

"I am Mouse, and I am
HIDING behind the CURTAINS!"

Miss Moon smiled. "Well dear," she said,
"now that we know
WHO you are
and
WHERE you are . . .

. . . why don't you come out
so that everyone can see you?"

Now, Mouse's mother had said to Mouse,
"Be sure to be good," so Mouse sighed,
and crept out from behind the curtain.

"That was a brilliant
hiding trick," said Bat.

"When I hide,"
said Owl,
"bits of me stick out."

"Me too," said Cat,
"and I have to remember
not to purr."

"I LIKE hiding,"
said Mouse.

"I know what,"
said Miss Moon . . .

PLANTS OF MAGIC

FIRST SPELLS

SPELLS v2

HISTORY OF MAGIC

SPELLS v3

" . . . let's play hide-and-seek
right now.
We've just got time
before midnight snacks."

Miss Moon closed
her eyes.

"12345678910"

"Coming!" she cried. "Ready or not!"

Miss Moon found Owl easily.

Quite a LOT of him was sticking out.

Miss Moon found Cat easily.

Cat was so pleased with her hiding place, she was purring rather loudly.

PURR PURR PURR PURR PURR

Miss Moon found Bat easily.

He had forgotten that
the fish tank was made
of glass and easy
to see through!

But Miss Moon
could not find
Mouse ANYWHERE.

"Mouse really is good at hiding,"
said Miss Moon.

"Let's all look for her."

So they looked inside
the paint pots . . .

. . . and they looked on the tops of cupboards
and they looked under a pile of special leaves.
But they couldn't find Mouse ANYWHERE.

"Oh dear," said Miss Moon.
"Mouse's mother WILL be cross
if we have lost her."

SPECIAL
LEAVES

Then Miss Moon
heard a tiny laugh.
"That sounds JUST like
Mouse," she said.

"Tee hee," Mouse laughed again.
"You didn't find ME!"

"That's true, dear," said Miss Moon,
"but now it's time for midnight snacks,
so do come out, and we can all
have something nice to eat."

Mouse crept out from her hiding place.
She had been hiding in Miss Moon's
hat-flowers all along!

"Well done, Mouse," said Miss Moon happily. "You are the best at hiding!"

And Owl and Bat and Cat all agreed.

Mouse
was SO pleased,
she forgot all
about being shy.

And she NEVER
hid from
her friends
again . . .

. . . unless, of course,
they were playing hide-and-seek.

Dedication

To my wife, Julie, and my boys, Kieran and Arun, who remind me of what's most important.

"In the plant, CO_2 and H_2O become ? BooBoo?" inquired Mr. Matheson.

"BooBoo!" he called again.

I stirred from my postprandial slumber, lifting my head from the table, reeling from my recent participation in a pig-fest that had taken place at the all-you-can-eat pizza place. I recalled the equation vaguely, but my mind was cluttered with the thought of vomiting the twenty-one and a half pieces of pizza I had just consumed.

"Well?" pressed Matheson.

"Glucose," I belched, and laid my head back down on the table.

I had done it! I was King of the Eating Team hands-down, and by a good half a piece of pizza too!

Little did I know the seeds that had been planted in my mind during my after-lunch biology class.

—FOR J. MATHESON AND THE BIOLOGY 300, CLASS OF '87

Preface

After completing *High-Yield Internal Medicine,* I had a profound sense that I had betrayed my specialty. After all, what is a surgical resident doing publishing a book about general medicine? Now that I have completed *High-Yield Surgery* (and, coincidentally, reached the end of my surgical residency training), I have realized that writing *High-Yield Internal Medicine* was the best thing I could have done for the sake of my training. After all, when we have completed our surgical residency training, we are given the degree of *Physician* and Surgeon.

Being a skilled surgeon involves more than just knowing how to do an operation. In fact, performing the operation is in many cases the easiest part of being a surgeon. The thoughts that keep skilled surgeons awake at night worrying involve which operation, if any, is best for the patient; how the patient will do postoperatively; and what measures can be taken to prevent the patient from experiencing complications.

This is the standpoint from which I have chosen to write *High-Yield Surgery*. My goal is to give readers a foundation with which to understand the art and science behind surgery, by providing them with the ability to understand the decision-making process that must occur whenever surgery is being contemplated, and describing specific indications for both surgical and less invasive therapies. I have specifically omitted detailed explanations of surgical procedures because these details should be emphasized later in one's surgical training. General practitioners and young surgical trainees will find this book useful for providing insight into when surgical referral is necessary and what the surgical specialty has to offer in terms of the treatment of specific disease processes.

The focus of this book is general surgery, including vascular, thoracic, and endocrine surgery. These areas are most likely to be incorporated into the general surgeon's practice, whether the practice is located in a major center or a rural setting. I have not addressed the surgical subspecialties—such as pediatric, cardiovascular, urologic, and orthopedic surgery—in this book because it would be difficult to cover the breadth of such material adequately, in this context. Further, while the general surgeon may obtain some experience in these specialties during training, it would be unusual for these specialties to be incorporated into a general surgeon's standard practice.

This second edition preserves the same focus as the first edition and highlights further developments in the surgical management of gastric, breast, and pancreatic diseases.

To future surgeons, remember—anyone can be taught to cut and tie, but the best surgeons know when not to operate.

R. Nirula, MD